# Cinderella: the terrible truth

By Laura North

Illustrated by Joelle Dreidemy

W
FRANKLIN WATTS
LONDON•SYDNEY

# Chapter 1

Have you heard the story about Cinderella?

The one where she wears rags and the Fairy

Godmother turns her into a pretty princess?

Well, it's all a big cover up.

That story hides the terrible truth.

Can you keep a secret?

It's true that Cinderella went to the famous Royal Ball.

"We've got an invitation for the Prince's Ball," said one of her stepsisters.

"Do you want to go Cinders dear? You can borrow my dress."

"That's nice of you sister!" said Cinderella, though she was surprised as her stepsisters were usually so unkind to her. She took the beautiful dress and put it on.

"Drink this Cinders," said her other stepsister.

"It's a love potion. It will make you even more beautiful and the Prince will fall in love with you."

Cinderella, who was very trusting, said, "Thank you sisters, you are so kind!"

She drank the potion in one go.

But her stepsisters were not kind. They were

cruel, mean and jealous of her beauty.

It was certainly not a love potion.

But what was it?

# Chapter 2

"We're here!" cried the stepsisters as they arrived at the palace with Cinderella. There was a full moon which lit up her beautiful blue dress. "You look wonderful."

"Wow!" said the Prince, as he stared

at Cinderella. "You are beautiful!"

Cinderella looked behind her. Surely the

Prince didn't mean her. But he dashed

straight up to her.

"The potion is working!" she thought.

"It has made me beautiful."

The Prince fell so madly in love with
her that he wanted to marry her
that very night.

"Cinderella – you must marry me now!
I cannot let you get away."

So they were wed straight away.

Cinderella became a princess.

The ball became a wedding party.

What could ruin such a perfect night?

# Chapter 3

"DONG! DONG! DONG!"

The clock struck midnight.

Outside, the big, round

full moon shone brightly.

But Cinderella's beautiful dress did not

turn back to rags. Instead, the potion

began its terrible work.

The Prince gazed deeply into the eyes of his
new love. "Cinderella," he said,
"You have such big, beautiful eyes."

"Oh Prince,
thank you,"
said Cinderella.

"Cinderella..." said the Prince, pausing, as he brushed his fingers over her hair. "You really do have tremendously big ears."

Cinderella liked the Prince, but his comments were getting a bit personal. "Well, Prince, I hadn't really noticed," she replied.

"Cinderella," said the Prince, now speaking very slowly. "I just hadn't noticed what great big teeth you have."

"Now, that's just rude," thought Cinderella.

But Cinderella thought that she should be polite to her new husband.

"It is so I can smile at you all the better," she told him. And she gave the biggest smile that she had ever given.

The Prince looked at her and screamed.
Cinderella called after the Prince
as he ran out of the Palace.

# Chapter 4

"What's happening?" cried Cinderella.

All around her, the guests were screaming.

"It's disgusting!" shouted one lady, pointing

at Cinderella. "Save us!"

"What's wrong?" asked Cinderella, moving
towards her. The woman screamed and
jumped out of the window into the moat.
In the night sky, the moon glowed
full and round.

A servant yelled,

"Look at those big, ugly feet!

And those terrible claws!"

Cinderella looked down.

Underneath her beautiful dress

a pair of huge, hairy feet poked out.

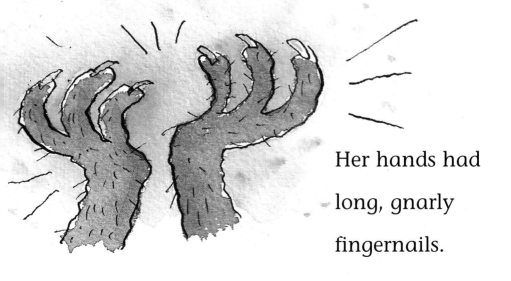

Her hands had

long, gnarly

fingernails.

She went to look in a mirror in the middle
of the ballroom.

"Help! I'm a monster!" she cried.

Her whole body was covered in thick hair,
and her face was furry with fierce fangs
and a snout. She was a werewolf!

"Not so pretty now, Cinders!" mocked
one of her stepsisters.

"And you thought it was a love potion!"

The sisters stopped laughing when

Cinderella leapt towards them.

When all the guests had run away,
Cinderella stood alone in the middle
of the ballroom and howled.

## Chapter 5

Five years later, Cinderella

sat locked in a cage.

"This is my prison,"

she said as she

looked at the bars.

But she was not alone.

The Prince sat

next to the cage.

"Well, we do have

to keep you locked up

when there's a full moon.

We don't want you to eat

any more of our relatives."

25

On the night of the ball, Cinderella had quickly gobbled up her two stepsisters.

The Prince still loved her. It was a shock to find out she was a werewolf. But he didn't mind a bit of hairiness and a bad temper.

"Daddy," said a small boy.

"Why is Mummy locked in a cage?"

"I'll tell you why when

you're a bit older, son," he said.

Around him lay their three children.

The Royal Family, however, wanted to keep it all a secret. So they made up a wonderful story about a Fairy Godmother,

a pumpkin

and a magic spell.

It was impossible to imagine that the truth was far stranger.

But I know the true story.

And now so do you.

Don't tell anyone else...

First published in 2012 by
Franklin Watts
338 Euston Road
London
NW1 3BH

Franklin Watts Australia
Level 17/207 Kent Street
Sydney
NSW 2000

Text © Laura North 2012
Illustration © Joelle Dreidemy

The rights of Laura North to be
identified as the author and Joelle Dreidemy
as the illustrator of this Work have been
asserted in accordance with the Copyright,
Designs and Patents Act, 1988.

Series Editor: Melanie Palmer
Series Advisor: Catherine Glavina
Series Designer: Peter Scoulding

A CIP catalogue record for this book is
available from the British Library.

ISBN 978 1 4451 0774 5 (hbk)
ISBN 978 1 4451 0780 6 (pbk)

Printed in China

Franklin Watts is a division of Hachette
Children's Books, an Hachette UK company.
www.hachette.co.uk